Rise of the Rebellion

Fiona Redred

CONTENTS

CHAPTER 1

T his is a recount of what happened to me and my friends on the 12th of Yaqui to the 32th of Yaqui in the year 759. This recount will be presented to the Chief of Pro-peace for the file ALISHA.

The 12th of Yaqui 759:

It was the day of the graduation. The day class 23s future would be decided. 38 of us sat in the exquisite Grand Hall praying that luck was on our side and we would be picked for our dream job. Me, Leo, Zara and Bane sat next to each other. We had all passed our exams with flying colours so hopefully we would all get into the Noxus Army aka NA.

The Headmaster walked out onto the temporary stage set up in the middle of the hall and began to speak. "Welcome Class 23," he said "It is an honour to have been you Head-master throughout your time at Kocsvo School for Young Fay. I hope you are satisfied with the jobs you get assigned to today. You have been assigned to a job that uses each of your individual skill sets. May the luck be on your side."

I glanced over at Leo and saw he was shaking, just slightly. Carefully I took his hand and squeezed it once, twice. Our secret code for its ok, I'm here. He gave my hand a squeeze then we both dropped the others hand. The NA recruitment officer had walked up to the podium and cleared his throat. This was it.

The moment me and my friends futures were decided. "It is with great happiness," he said. "That NA is welcoming 10 students from your class into its training program. Each student was handpicked for their skills across all subjects but with a focus on intelligence and combat skills. I hope you all find your preferred role in our glorious army during the training program."

It was at that moment I saw a figure moving outside the window. Odd, I thought then turned my attention back to the stage. "The following students have been excepted into the NA; Avery Stone, Harri Davidson, Arya Smith, Gus Cloud, Leo Dennis, Zara Wilson, Felix Stevenson, Bane Turner and ..."We never did find out who the last person was. CRACK!

A gunshot echoed around the room. The recruitment officer was thrown to his left as the bullet penetrated his chest. He fell to the ground with a thud. Everyone stood still for a second. Then everyone started screaming and running out of the room pushing each other to get out of danger. I shouted over to my gang," GET TO THE STAGE!"

Leo and Zara jumped out of their seats closely followed by Bane. I took the lead as we dodged panicking civilians and sprinted to the stage. As I closed in on the fallen officer I caught a glimpse of his face. It couldn't be, I thought. But it was. It was Officer Volta. The head of the FA. By the time all this had gone through my head I was next to Volta. Me and Zara knelt down beside him as Leo and Bane covered us.

Zara grabbed the med-pac she had stashed somewhere about her person. I ripped Zoltas parade shirt open and put both my hands over the wound. I knew it was too little to late though. After a pool of blood gets to a certain size nothing will help. Bane shouted," Security's coming!" Zara slammed a field dressing over the bullet wound. The look on her face said it all. "We're going to lose him." she mumered.

Zolta made a jerky movement with his head and gurgled," Th Hadlrd s vil."I lent closer to his head trying to catch what he was trying to say, leaving Zara to attend to his wound. "The Shadowlord is evil," he spluttered, pink blood foaming around his mouth as he tried to speak," You have to stop him. Find Alisha. They hold the key to defeating...."Zoltas head flopped backwards and his eyes went blank. Zara took her hands of his wound and shook her head. "He's gone.""YOU ARE UNDER ARREST FOR MURDER!" Security shouted. "Fuck," Leo swore.

"RUN!!" I screamed. If what Zolta had said to me was true then we were in immediate danger and needed to run fast. Me and Zara left to our feet and started sprinting in the direction of the fire exit with Bane and Leo. Leo, I thought. Why was I thinking about Leo right now?! It wasn't helpful was it?! An alarm sounded bringing me back to the present. Bane was holding the fire door open shouting "Go, go, go!!"

The gang bolted through the red door and Bane slammed it shut behind us, flexing his biceps. Leo, Bane and Zara opened their mouths simultaneously but I stopped the barrage of questions with," No time to explain, we need to go to a safe house, I will explain there but for now you just have to trust me ok, 1000 laps." 1000 laps was our code for please trust me if Im wrong I will do 1000 running laps. In training we all hated laps so doing 1000 was torture. Everyone nodded.

We zoomed round the side of the building to the hover park. Luckily for us Zara had turned 18 a few months before and had her own hover now. The rest of us were still 17 and to young to drive. As we piled into Zara's electric blue hover (which really was only made to fit 3 but we weren't to concerned about breaking that particular law and anyway sitting on Leo's lap wasn't the worst experience in the world) we heard the sounds of Security closing in on us. Zara put her foot down and we started to speed away from Security, through the gaps in the crowd of people and towards safety.

Well somewhere safer than here. I don't think we were safe anywhere anymore.

We eventually arrived at the safe house. It was an old building that had been abandoned years ago and no one had found it yet. We pulled up in the driveway and hid the hover under some tarps. Opening the door we piled inside before anyone could see us. As we stood, panting in the sitting room I opened my mouth to speak then Bane sighed," Can we sit down first Arya?"I sat down on the purple couch Zara had put there last month. Everyone else sat down around me.

"Ok," I explained," This is going to sound ridiculous but when Zolta was dying he told me something."I paused for a second waiting to gauge their reactions. "Well tell us," Bane prompted."Zolta told me that the Shadowlord is evil. I was told to find someone called Alisha apparently they are the only person able to stop him. That was Zolta's dying words." "Well then," Leo proclaimed," Let's find this Alisha person whoever they are.""Yes I agree," Zara said."Let's do this!" Bane shouted.

So it was decided. Everyone agreed that we should follow the Alisha lead. Bane discovered that Zolta lived in a town called Serilia on the east coast. It was about a day's driving from the safe house which was on the outskirts of Xati. We were going to travel there tomorrow and start looking for clues about who Alisha was.

Tonight though, we were going to crash at the safe house so we were well rested for tomorrow. It was a fairly big house, build back in the Cariva era when we were ruled by a democracy. Me and Leo were going to share the twin room while Bane and Zara would have single rooms to themselves. Zara gave me a look when me and Leo said we were happy to share the twin but we are strictly friends. I think.

That night, after we ate burgers for dinner, the gang turned in for the night. Me and Leo said goodnight to Zara and Bane then walked up the stairs to the twin room on the 2nd floor. As we closed the door behind us Leo sighed," What are we going to do Arya?""What do you mean??""We're trying to take down the fucking monarch! It's four of us against the an whole army!""I never said you lot had to take part in this plan Leo.""True. But why would I let my best friend do this by herself?""I... I.... I don't..... I don't know.""Exactly."

I had barely put my bag on the floor next to my bed when Leo tugged his shirt over his head. I went bright red as I tried not to look at his body and well..... failed. Miserably. I couldn't tear my eye's away from the six pack on his stomach...the way his pecs flexed as he folded his arms and.... spoke.

"Am I really that good looking?" he smirked."Umm... well.. yes but I wasn't looking because.. I was just surprised that's all.""Ok," he smiled," I believe you, millions wouldn't.""Ok."I didn't have any pyjamas with me so I turned round and pulled my tunic dress over my head so i was just wearing my crop shirt and mini shorts. Turning back round I saw Leo had gotten into bed and was lying down with his eyes closed. Quietly as possible I climbed into my bed and pulled the covers up around my neck.

I lay still for what seemed like forever. My watch went from 10pm to 11pm to 11:30pm. Then just as I was away to give up on getting any sleep whatsoever something happened. As the clock hit midnight I heard Leo throw back his covers and swing his feet onto the floor. He walked over to my bed and tapped me on the shoulder. "Arya are you awake?" he murmured. "Yes," I whisper. "Can I sleep in your bed? I can't sleep tonight." "I'm the same. Get in."

Leo lay down next to me. After a few seconds I rolled over to face him and snuggled up against his chest. He put his arm round me and pulled me closer. Within minutes we were asleep. To this day i don't know why Leo got up at midnight. Why he decided to potentially wake me just to fall asleep next to me. That night was the best night's sleep of my life.

Chapter 2

The 13th of Yaqui 759:

The morning after me and Leo shared a bed I woke up at 7 am. I rolled over expecting Leo to be there but there was just a warm spot where his body had been. Sleepy, I dragged myself out of bed and started to head to the bathroom, with the hope of freshening up before we set of for Serilia. As I blundered into the bathroom, rubbing my eyes, I walked straight into Leo. "Oof," he grunted, "Way to say good morning Arya." "Sorry," I replied, "Didn't know you were in here." "I've just finished shaving and I'm away to start packing. Want me to do yours as well?" "Please." "Ok then. See you at breakfast."

It was in that moment just then that I could've said something. What I would have said, I don't know. But it would only have taken a small tilt of my head and we would have been kissing. Then the moment passed and we walked off in opposite directions to go get ready for the day. As I splashed water on my face and did my hair I pondered where today would take us.

Up in till less than 24 hours ago I had my whole life planned out. Now I was on the run from the NA and following some half baked instructions from a dying man. I must be mad I thought to myself. Sitting around the breakfast table we discussed what would happen today. The plan was this; We would leave at 9am, in an hour in a half. The drive to Serilia would take roughly 10 hours so we arrive just after 7pm all being well. Zara had a old friend who was going to house us for a week at most. With any luck Alisha would be easy to find and we wouldn't need to stay the entire week. Hopefully.

After breakfast I helped Zara pack. We were nearly finished putting together a selection of basic weapons in a case when she said "So what happened between you and Leo last night hmm?""Nothing happened Zara.""Right.""We shared a bed that's all. We're just friends.""I've seen the way you look at him. That ain't just friends.""So maybe I like him. He's not into me and never will be. I'm happy to have him as just a friend."Zara looked like she was away to say something in reply but at that moment Leo and Bane ran outside with the last of the cases, whooping "Road trip!" Throwing the cases into the boot of the hover we piled in and with Zara driving, Leo in the passenger seat and me and Bane crammed in the back we were off.

2 hours into the trip and tensions were starting to gain height. 4 people in a hover meant for 3 isn't ideal conditions for a long haul drive and this trip was full of nerves and paranoia as we were all stressing about getting pulled over. Bane was starting to complain about cramps so we pulled over to the side of the little country road and fell out the hover. I opened up my bag and pulled out a couple of sandwiches that we devoured as we walked up and down the road.

It was clear to me that Zara and Leo were both trying to speak to me privately, I knew Zara's reason, Leo's on the other hand, wasn't obvious. I made sure that we didn't end up in a position we could have that chat though. The last thing we needed was to complicate this whole shitfest with my stupid feelings I may or may not have for Leo. We hadn't spoken directly since we slept together last night. I wondered what he was thinking right now. I just couldn't guess.

"Arya? Arya!"A shout brought me back to the present. Bane was calling my name. "We're setting off again Arya! We need to get to Serilia before sundown you know!""Ok!" I shouted back, starting to jog towards the car. Before long we were back on the road speeding towards Serilia and hopefully, some answers to this mystery.

At some point I must have fallen asleep, despite it being the middle of the afternoon. When I can round again it was because Leo whispered, "Arya, we're just entering Serilia," into my ear. I jerked awake, accidentally head butting the roof of the hover as I sat bolt upright. "Woah, careful," Leo soothes, "We can't have you hurting yourself now, can we?" I nodded, surprised he's suddenly so caring towards me.

Maybe Zara and Bane had a word with him while I was asleep. I wouldn't put it past Zara to do that. She's very loyal to her friends. As the lights of the town engulfed us in their sea of advertising and neon signs for different clubs, I felt weirdly detached from reality. Like I was watching my life from a strangers point of view. Shaking my head to clear my brain I start to properly taking in my surroundings. Training kicking in, I quickly started to gain my bearings. We were on the east side of town heading towards the infamous Street Luck. It was on Street Luck that the dealers ran their business, that the gangs ruled the streets and more importantly, don't ask, don't tell was rule No.1.

We drove halfway down the road before turning off onto a side street. Passing signs for a variety of motels and hostels we pulled into a small parking lot. Clambering out the hover we sleepily took our cases from the boot and dragged them round to the front of a motel named The Shining Star. As we open the door, struggling with the greasy handle, a voice said, "Name for booking?" "Zara Wilson, 4 people, 2 double rooms." Zara mumbled. "3rd floor, rooms 3R and 3Q." "Thanks."

We stumbled upstairs, to tired to talk. Almost on autopilot Zara and Bane took 3R and me and Leo took 3Q. Leo got changed as I did my teeth and then we switched. Climbing into the double bed, I waited for Leo to come through and get to bed. I didn't expect that Leo would cuddle me again tonight. But he did. Tangled together, we drifted off, full of anticipation for the next day.

CHAPTER 3

The 14th of Yaqui 759:

In the morning I woke up to the sound of a old fashioned, non magical alarm clock ringing. Groaning, I rolled over to hit snooze but instead hit something soft and warm that definitely wasn't the alarm. It took me a few seconds to register that I whacked Leo's bare chest instead! I was shocked by how toned his muscles were but I quickly snatched my hand away, embarrassed.

After successfully turning the alarm off I attempted to wake Leo up. He sleeps like a baby, I thought as I unsuccessfully tried to shake him awake. Giving up on that technique I resorted to filling a bottle full of cold water and squirting it over his face. He awoke with a start, yelling, "Da fuck are you doing that for Trisha!?" I was stunned.

Who was Trisha? Was she his gf? If so why hadn't Leo mentioned her? The thought that Leo was keeping secrets from me stung more than it should have. Then I remembered.

Trisha was his younger sister who was in 2nd year at the Academy. Why my mind had instantly jumped to conclusions worried me. I said, "It's me Arya. Time to get up sunshine!" Masking my previous panic with a cheery tone and smile, I grabbed his arm and dragged him out of the bed onto the floor. And so the day began.

I found a somewhat decent outfit from the clothes in my suitcase (cargos, crop shirt, leather jacket and trainers). After getting dressed my focus turned to trying to tame my hair. As it hang down to my lower back I decided to brush the blue locks and braid them together. Leo stood by the door, tapping his foot as he started to lose patience. "Finally," he rolled his eyes, grinning, "Let's go get breakfast. The others will be waiting."

"I only took 10 minutes longer than you, who may I remind you, wouldn't wake up this morning!" I retaliated."Sure babes." He replied, smirking.BABES!!!! My head practically exploded with surprise. Maybe Leo did like me after all. Or maybe it was a joke. A offhand comment. Sarcasm. Yes, I think. It must have been sarcasm. I didn't get time to torture myself further as at that moment the door exploded inwards, Bane yelling," Get up you lazy little...!" before realising we weren't in fact, still asleep but actually awake and dressed. Zara walked in behind him.

"Epic fail Bane. The 'lazy shits' as you put it, are fully aware and prepared." She laughed, throwing her head back. "Whatever," muttered Bane, clearly disgruntled about being wrong. Laughing, we headed out of the motel to grab breakfast from a 'great little bakery that does the best moon cakes' according to Leo. No one argued about moon cakes for breakfast.

The bakery in question was actually only 10 minutes down the road. We walked there in silence, heads down, fearing being spotted, despite it being this side of town. The door opened with a tinkling noise as the bell rang. Breathing in, you could smell delicious aromas of all sorts of savoury and sweet treats. Leo was right, I thought. This certainly seemed like the best bakery in Serilia.

Looking around the shelves I thought I might never be able to pick. Eventually I picked a blood orange moon cake (£2) and a chocolate pretzel (£4). I paid for everyone using cash I got from the bank the day before graduation. In total we spent £20 on breakfast."Won't your parents mind you're spending all their cash?" Asked Zara."Nah I doubt they'll even notice. It's not like they ever pay much attention to their bank accounts or me." I replied with a sigh. Sometimes I wonder if I would've been a better person if my stupid rich parents had taken care of me, instead of leaving me with a string of au pairs while they travelled.

"That kinda sucks." Leo mummered. "Agreed." Bane said as he picked up the bagged groceries."Anyhow it's lucky for us because we have in total, £2980 left to use!" I exclaimed, plastering a smile across my face.

Back at the motel we made our plans for the day. We would split into 2 groups; me and Bane and Zara and Leo. Leo looked uncomfortable about this decision but didn't say anything. Zara and Leo have always been.... odd. You wouldn't be able to notice it most of the time but sometimes, like just now it shows through. Something to do with their older siblings I believe but I don't know the details and have never asked. Maybe today is a chance for them to sort it all out.

I zoned back in wondering how much I had missed. The general consensus was this; Leo and Zara would stake out Zoltas now empty house, in preparation for a break in tomorrow night. Meanwhile me and Bane would gather as much information on Zolta as possible to try and figure out who assassinated him. We were to also check up on the Shadowlord's lastest news conferences and see if we could find anything interesting ie edited videos, misleading information, etc.

The bibliotheca we wanted to visit was in the centre of town ages away from the motel. As it was already 9 o'clock me and Bane decided to take the train into town and walk the remaining 15 minutes to get to the bibliotheca. Zara needed to take a different route to get to Zoltas house so we parted ways at the lobby. "Be good you two," smiled Zara. "I don't want to have to pick you up from the police station at midnight because you did something silly.""Same goes for you." I retorted.

"But we're not the ones who got stupid drunk at prom and got arrested." Smirked Leo, sure he had won this. "That wasn't strictly me and Banes fault. We didn't know that Blue Winds are hella strong but don't taste it." I replied. "Anyhow," Bane interjected just as Leo opened his mouth to comment, "We all have places to be so I suggest we get a move on. Meet back here at.... 7pm tonight?" "Agreed." We all replied.

After final goodbyes we parted ways for the day. Me and Bane engaged in light conversation as we walked towards the station. When we finally reached the bottom of the steps I was shocked. There wasn't any sort of Wanted posters with our faces on it anywhere in sight. Half relieved, half concerned I bought tickets for the two of us and we climbed onto the shuttle. As it started to pull out of the station, the levitation lines humming, I had that strange feeling that I was being watched. But when I turned around, no one was there.

CHAPTER 4

The 14th of Yaqui 759

As we stepped of the train into the bright sunshine and lush green plants of the town centres station I couldn't help thinking about the careful, nurtured world that the rich grow up in, such a contrast to the slums of Serilia. Bane caught my hand and started to lead me along. I realised I had stopped slap in the middle of the station entrance. Stumbling a little as Bane tugged my arm I hurried to catch him up.

Walking into the bibliotheca I took a deep breath in, savouring the smell of old books. Bane looked at me like I was mad but let me have my moment. Then the hunt for anything vaguely related to Alisha and Zolta began. I took the non fiction section, while Bane checked out the digital newspaper archives. "Remember," I whispered," If anyone asks where doing research for our History test on the NA.""Roger that," Bane replied.I gave a thumbs up to Bane and turned to go to the non fiction section as he sat down at one of the databases.

Magical History. Maybe we would find something interesting there...

CHAPTER 5

1 4th of Yaqui 759:

Inside the Museum of Magical History was the biggest collection of magical objects and information in all of Noxus. Bane held open the door for me, bowing as he smirked, "This way Your Highness.""Thank you, peasant." I grinned.Glaring at me he closed the door behind us and we walked up to the visitors desk."What can I do for you two today?" A smiling receptionist asked.

"Two 5 hour passes please." I said brightly."Do you want vault access as well? It gives you an exclusive access to the historical records for only £5.99 each."I glanced at Bane, wondering weather the extra expense was worth it. He nodded slightly and said, "How far back do the available records go?""The records go back to the beginning of the glorious Shadowlord's regime.""Thank you. We'll take that offer." Bane smiled graciously."Ok that will be £30 for the pair of you."

After we finally got in (Bane went mental at the price of the passes) we decided to do all the research we could on groups of wielders and magic stripping. Banes finds earlier had led us to believe if we stripped the Shadowlord of his magic he would die. The only problem was neither of us had taken Magical Studies past 1st year and therefore had no idea what the process of magic stripping involved. Neither of us could contact Zara or Leo to pick their brains (they both had taken Magical Studies to 4th year) and as we had left our mobiles at the dorms before graduation none of us had phones anymore.

Bane wanted to read about the powers of groups of wielders so I was stuck with magic stripping and everything it involved. Magical Studies was my worst class so I was definitely going to have to write everything down for Zara or Leo to read later. Ugh. My brain already hurt even though I hadn't even got to the vaults yet. Bane found the exhibit he needed to look at and ran off. Possibly because there was a large interactive section with several computers. He is such a nerd, I thought. Sighing I turned left, following the signage to the vaults.Maybe I would find something useful this time, unlike in the bibliotheca. Which was, in my opinion, a major waste of time.

Going round yet another corner I groaned. The vaults were being guarded by 2 burly security guards, exactly the sort who get a kick out of playing like Pro-peace Officers. Oh great, I thought, idiots with guns just what I need today. Right on cue the slightly bigger one shouted, "What are you doing here!" at me.

"I want to access the records." I stated firmly. "Does the lickle wickle girly wanna access the big scwary records?" The other guard said, laughing as he mocked my slight Northern accent. "Yes I do. I have paid for this privilege so please let me in." I was getting angry now but tried to remain calm. "We'll need to see proof of admission to let you in." Guard 1 patronised. I gritted my teeth. I hated being baby talked. "Ok. Here's my pass. As you can see, I paid for access so if you don't have reason to suspect me, please let me in or I will file a complaint." I was at my wits end with these bozos as I handed over the pass.

They spent far too long inspecting the pass, fussing over every small detail. Eventually Guard 2 opened the door and still mocking me said, "Have fun looking through the big books." I muttered a thank you dickhead under my breath. Luckily they didn't hear otherwise I think they might've had me thrown out. Last thing we need is a brush with the authorities today.

Now I could properly concentrate on my work. As far as I was aware I was the only person down here and that meant I could look through the records in peace and quiet. I looked along the shelving units until I found Wielders, Magic. Rolling the shelving until I could fit in the gap, I walked down the aisle, skimming my fingers over the different articles and books. I breathed in, the air thick with the scent of old paper. Pulling a couple of interesting looking pieces from the shelves I walked over to one of the tables, propping up the book on the stand. I removed my notes from my purse along with a pen and sat down. Opening the first book I sat down, ready to lose myself in the contents...

I don't know how much time passed as I read through the records I pulled and scribbled page after page of notes on everything I could possibly find that might be relevant. Spells, chants, different powers, practically everything magic related went on the sheets of notes. Leo would kill me later for giving him and Zara so much work but oh well. It was worth it to be prepared. And maybe, just maybe, the magic stripping would take down the Shadowlord. Hopefully. I heard a massive thump and jumped, mind shooting back to when I heard the gun go off at graduation. Luckily it was only the top few books falling off the pile. Sighing I got up and put them back in their respective places. As I did so I swore I could've heard footsteps that weren't my own.

Shrugging it off as paranoia due to the badly lit vaults I finished putting the books back. Wandering back to the table my work was on my mind started to wonder why the Shadowlord had turned evil. We had lived in a dictatorship for as long as I could remember but one of the au pairs my parents had hired told me about the democracy.

Sitting on the couch, cuddled up against her soft folds of skin, listening to how at the beginning of the Shadowlords time as a politician he had been one of the kindest, most respectful people in the Senate.But over the years he changed. Became colder, with scandal after scandal attached to him. Still people loved him. Elected him President after only 5 years. He was horrible by then, listening to none of the Senate councillors. The next year the Senate was dissolved and the once prosperous nation of Noxus descended into a regime with basically no international communication.

I finally came closer to my table, relief flooding through me that I was still alone down here. A few minutes after I sat down however, I heard footsteps again. Peering out into the huge space the vaults inhabited, I didn't see anyone. The glow from my desk lamp only stretched a few feet into the darkness though. Time passed and I thought I had been imagining things when I heard the footsteps again and felt a cold hand on my shoulder...

CHAPTER 6

The 14th of Yaqui 759:

I let out a high pitched scream, convinced that I was being arrested. Instinct took over and I twisted round in my chair, slapping whoever it was in the face. Hard. "The fuck Arya?!" Bane cried, hand going to his face. "It's me, calm down!""Bane you little canis! I thought you were a Pro-peace officer!" "Of course it's me! Now shush, someone might hear us."

"It's your fault I screamed." I said, disgruntled that he had scared me so badly."Ok I will take the blame for that." He concedes after a minute."Good.""More to the point it's no w..." He checks his watch. "5:30 and our train leaves at 6 so I suggest we get going if we want to avoid the wrath of Zara.""Oh yeh we should leave. How did your research go?""Good but not as good as yours by the looks of things." He said, shooting a pointed glance at the stack of notes on my desk."Yep probably."

Hurriedly I packed my notes away, fearing missing the train. We walked out of the vaults into the main building. I had to blink a few times as I adjusted to the brightly lit displays. The vaults had been in semi darkness the entire time I was down there. It was much quieter in the museum now, as it was close to closing time and all the families and school trips had long since returned home. The girl on the visitor desk thanked us for visiting and told us to come again. I certainly hope we can. One day. Maybe me and Leo can visit together. My mind drifted off into fantasy land and I zoned out of the present.

I was jolted back to the moment by the blare of a loud-speaker. We were at the station now and I stared at the departures board to find our train. It was on time thank the Goddess. I signalled to Bane that we should sit down on some of the benches while we wait for our train to arrive. Fighting my way through the rich hour crowd I found two seats next to each other, relived, me and Bane flopped down onto them. "I wonder how Zara and Leo got on." I pondered out loud."Hopefully fairly well, we need that info to get into the house." Bane replied."True.

I just hope no one caught them." I fretted."They'll be fine it's Zara and Bane for crying out loud." He comforted."Still I worry about him." I caught my mistake the second it was out my mouth and I knew from Banes expression I had some explaining to do."You worry about Leo?" His voice gave away nothing."Well... yes but... it's not what..." My voice stumbled over the words."So you worry about him but it's platonic?"" No... I... I don't want to but I like him."

"For fucks sakes Arya he's into you! You two flirt all the time!""That's just how Leo is. Besides we've got bigger problems than my feelings. If we all survive this then I'll address that issue.""He can be like that but... It seems different with you. That's a good plan though.""Yeh." I reply, not sure where the conversation should go next.

We sit in an awkward silence for what seems like forever. Just as I remember about the waitress in the cafe and what I wanted to ask Bane the train pulls in. Jumping up from the bench we hurried on board the train and found some seats close to the door. The scent of stress and tiredness seeps up my nose as the train filled up with over-worked, sleep deprived office workers returning home to their families.

I glance over to the announcement boards, hoping to see that this trip will be over soon. Instead I see an all too familiar photo. Or make that photos. Me, Leo's, Banes and Zara's senior year portraits are splashed on the board with a caption of 'Wanted! For murder and treason. £10000 reward for any one of them alive.' Fucking shit, I think. Subtly nudging Bane, I motion towards the board. He lets out a hiss of breath followed by a whispered, "We're fucked."

I simply nodded in reply, too scared to speak out loud, lest someone realise who we are. The train suddenly seemed too crowded. The chances that we would get arrested went through the roof as more and more people saw the screen. Some people were even photoing it and for the looks of it, posting it on their social media accounts. I kept my head down and prayed. If If we got arrested now we would have let the Shadowlord win. That can't happen. We have to find Alisha.

After what seemed like eternity the train pulled into the station. I practically jumped out my seat, eager to be away from the crowds. Bane was close behind as I left the crowds of people and burst out into the street. I started running in the direction of the motel, hoping against hope that the others hadn't been caught. "Slow down Arya!" Banes voice rang out. "I can't keep up!"I skidded to a halt, gulping air down to catch my breath."Hey, hey, it's going to be ok." He comforted."I hope so.

The signs though... it... it scared me more than it should have.""I agree. It was out of the blue and we were stuck in a tin can with people who could have had us arrested.""Yeh." I breathed shakily. The adrenaline rush was wearing off and all I want to do now was see Zara and Leo."Come on, let's get back to the motel before Zara freaks. It's already 6:45." "Ok."

Getting to the motel didn't take long, considering I had sprinted half the way there. The lobby was still lit by a single fluorescent light that flickered as we walked through the door. Me and Bane didn't speak as we climbed the stairs to our floor. We were both thinking the same thing. What if Zara and

Leo got caught? I knew I shouldn't worry. Leo was a genius in the field, always top of our class in the Academy.The clock struck 7 as we walked into Bane and Zara's room.

"Bang on time." Bane commented as he pulled his notes out and put them on the table. "Where's Zara and Leo though?" I wondered. We had agreed to be back for 7 and they weren't here. Taking a deep breath I turned to the window, peering through the grime onto the street below. "No sign of either of them." I announced. "Typical. One rule for us, another for the all mighty Zara." Bane sighed. I had to agree slightly though. Zara was most definitely the mother of our friend group. In that sense Bane was the rebel middle child, Leo was the sporty eldest child and I was... I don't know what I was actually. Maybe the rich aunt.

Time passed. Still no sign of Leo and Zara. Even Bane, who could remain calm in an earthquake, was starting to visibly stress. At half past I ordered dinner from the motel kitchen. It was too risky to be going out regularly, even in this part of town. Me and Bane got a Sushi plate to share and Bibimbap and Pad Thai for Leo and Zara respectively. The food arrived about 10 minutes later. Me and Bane tucked in, unsure what had happened to the others. Just as we finished eating the pair of them burst into the room, panting heavily. "We have a lot to discuss." Zara told us at the same time Leo said, "Yum Bibimbap!"

CHAPTER 7

The 15th of Yaqui 759:

I woke up in Leo's arms. This was becoming a regular occurrence and that was worrying. I couldn't let myself get too attached anyone, not when I might have to make a life or death decision to ensure the downfall of the Shadowlord. Leo rolled over, releasing me from his hug. It was clear the he was fast asleep as he was snoring softly.

Checking the time I realised it was only 6am. Groaning, I swung my legs out of bed and onto the scratchy carpet. There was no point trying to cram in an extra hour of sleep now so I busied myself in getting up and ready for the day. As I brushed my teeth I pondered over what Leo and Zara had said last night. It was certainly a lot to think about. After they had finished shovelling food down their throats me and Bane got the explanation that we had been dying to hear.

It went something like this. Leo and Zara had successfully done a stake out of Zoltas house and were confident they had the codes to get in tonight. There wasn't much activity apparently, just a few housekeeping staff who left at 6 and a visit by the Captain, who only stayed half an hour or so. As far as we could tell, the place was a dead zone for tourists, which had an upside and and a downside. The upside was that no-one should see us unexpectedly but the downside is that we would stick out like a sore thumb. Hopefully thought, today we could make a foolproof plan for the heist and we would find Alisha sometime tomorrow.

A loud thud shocked me out of my thoughts. At first I wondered if someone had ratted us out and that was Pro-Peace knocking down the door. Hurriedly I spat out the toothpaste and put my brush down, preparing to fight or flee. That theory was discarded though as I heard a groan and, "Fuck that hurt," in a sleepy tone. I poked my head out the bathroom. Leo was lying on the floor, wrapped up in a duvet."Did you fall out of bed?" I asked in a sweet voice, designed to annoy people. "What do you think?" He replied."That you did." "Correct." He grumbled."Do you need help?""No..... yes.""Ok."

I sauntered over, enjoying the moment of superiority. I smirked down at Leo before stretching out my hand to help him up. He took it, stumbling to his feet. "Idiot," I said fondly. "Dumbass," he replied. "I'm not trying to be rude but how did you fall out of bed?""I rolled over onto the floor. It's how normal people fall out of bed Arya." Leo sighed, tussling my hair. He disappeared into the bathroom without another word. And so our day began.

It turns out we had woken up around 10am so by the time we had sat down to discuss plans for the day, it was at 11:30, over brunch. "So," Bane prompted, "How quiet are we planning to break into a - sorry - the highest security house in Serilia without getting caught?""Well," began Zara, "We know the codes for the gate and the back door so getting in to the actual building should be ok. The 2 guards walk around the perimeter and it takes them 50 minutes to do that so the guards come by every 25 minutes. CCTV is mainly fake or powered off.""Basically the house is only on high security mode when Zoltas home, which he obviously isn't." Leo summarised in between bites of his pain au chocolat. "Perfect!" I exclaimed."So the plan is?" Bane said.

Zara was quiet for a minute while she finished her mouthful of bread. Finally she swallowed and said, "Leo can explain he's the tech expert here, not me.""Ok," said Leo, "So we get to the house at 2200 hours. Getting in to the grounds should be quite quick and if I'm right we will have another 20 min to get to the back door before security comes round again.

Once we're inside there isn't really any sort of a plan so open to suggestions."Everyone was silent for a minute while we complemented what the best course of action was. Finally Bane spoke up. "There's got to be a floor plan for the building right? From before it was Zoltas house?""Yep, it's online, I can't guarantee it's still accurate though." Leo told us."No it will be because it was a protected site they couldn't have changed the layout that much." Zara interjected.The conversation continued like this for a while longer as we ironed out the details.

Finally at sometime around 12 we finished finalising the plan. It was this. We would get there for 2200 hours and be inside by 2230. There was 3 different locations that Zolta could've stored confidential information in; the study, the library and the safe. We didn't have the combination for the safe but Leo was confident that him and Bane could crack it.

We would be out again by 2315 hours and home and safe, hopefully with the documents about Alisha in tow. Now all we had left to do was sit and wait. We soon got bored of waiting and me and Zara decided to leave the boys at the motel and go for a walk. Leo whined for a bit about it until he realised he could go and practice his parkour at the hoverboard park opposite the motel. Bane kindly agreed to accompany him so no one was left on their own.

There wasn't much ,well any, woodland near Serilia but there was the beach and harbour. Me and Zara strolled down to the beach, engaging in a bit of light conversation. Both of us were cautious about not being recognised by anyone as the 2 girls from the Koscvo graduation attack, as the news had taken to calling it.

Once we made it down onto the beach we relaxed as it wasn't busy in the slightest. There was a silence as we both struggled for words. Zara broke it by saying, "Look! There's whales!" She was pointing out to sea, and clear as day, there was a pod of whales breaching the surface. We stood in silence watching them frolic in the sun. It was a beautiful sight, especially before we had to do something dangerous tonight. They eventually disappeared and we turned to walk back to the motel, both feeling, well, different than before. More magical perhaps.

CHAPTER 8

The 15th of Yaqui 759:

The butterflies in my stomach were about to break free and fly away. We were crouched outside the gate to Zoltas house, waiting for the guards to walk by so we could punch in the code. I shifted my weight, trying to stop my leg going to sleep. The footsteps gradually faded into the distance as they moved by us, unaware that the biggest security threat in the entirety of their careers was sitting mere meters away. Confident that we were out of earshot Leo crept forward and punched a 4-digit code into the keypad.

The gate pinged open, swinging to one side to reveal a long winding driveway. With Zara in the lead we hurry up the driveway towards the gardens, wincing when our shoes crunched the gravel underfoot. Luckily the guards were far enough away that they didn't hear us. I breathed a huge sigh of relief when Bane stepped onto the lawn. Now we only had to get into the back door and find the files. It was 2215 hours.

Padding softly through the grass we kept close the bushes of the exterior wall, hiding in their shadows as the moon shone down on us. Leo whispered, "The back door should be just on the other side of this flowerbed.""Ok." Came the reply from the rest of us.

He was right as well and within 5 minutes we were poised ready to enter the house. While Leo was fiddling with the lock Bane said, "Ok guys me and Zara will take the study, Leo, you and Arya can take the library. Meet at the safe for 2250.""Hang on I thought me and Zara were a team?!" I responded, confused."Change of plans." I would've argued more but it was at that moment the lock slid back, opening the door. Zara made a 'Go, Go, Go" sign and we hurried inside, propping the door open behind us. I looked back at Bane, begging him with my eyes to change the teams. He dropped eye contact and I turned to follow Leo upstairs.

The back stairs in Zoltas mansion was comparable to the grand staircase at Kocsvo. They stretched up to a stately landing then split in two towards the second floor. Luckily for us there was signs pointing to various different rooms including but not limited to; The Master Bedroom, The Movie Theatre and most importantly, The Library. This sign pointed up the left hand staircase, so I took the lead and hurried upstairs, careful to stay as quiet as possible.

The library was straight across the hall from the stairs. Leo, eager as a puppy, bounded over to the double oak doors and pulled them both at once. The doors stayed closed as he overbalanced. I ran over and caught him before he hit the floor, arms tucked under his.

"I think it's a push door." He said sarcastically."Really?" I replied. "Yeh."Now I was aware of how close our body's were. I put Leo back on his feet and stepped round him to push the door open. No point wasting any more time fussing when we had a job to do. Inside the library was 3 full walls of books split into sections, a few chairs and 2 large desks with book stands on them.

Seeing the desks as a good place to start my hunt, I walked over and opened the first drawer. Out of the corner of my eye I saw Leo do the same with the other desk. There were a few papers in the drawer so I flipped through them. It all seemed to be notes on a book called The Tragedy of Lacy Gray. I was pretty sure we read that for 5th year Common and after a quick read of the papers realised that we did and Zolta was writing fan fiction for it.

The rest of the desk revealed nothing apart from Zolta was an avid reader and writer. Leo's desk had similar results, but contained a document on erasing magic that was pocketed for further reading."I wonder if he hid something in one of the books?" Leo wondered aloud."It would take too long to search them all we only have 15 minutes." Came my reply."One of the sections is called Favourites though.""Your point?""If I were hiding documents I would keep them somewhere so obvious no on3 would ever think to look."

He strode over to the shelf and peered at the books. "Hey look at this." Leo called. "Ssshhh!" I said, "Someone might hear us! What is it though?" "The dust patterns. One of them is covered in dust. My guess is it hasn't been touched in ages." I stopped beside him and realised he was right. Taking the book off the shelf, I thumbed through it until three sheets of paper floated down to the floor. Leo picked them up and scanned over each one as I placed the book back on the shelf.

Craning my neck to see over his shoulder I caught the words Fuiki, Tower and Resistance. "These aren't about Alisha." Leo hissed. "Great." I replied. "They look useful let's take them." "Was going to."

Just then I checked the time and realised that we needed to hurry to meet Bane and Zara at the safe. 5 minutes later, we stood around the safe pondering how to get in. They hadn't found any documents on Alisha and I was starting to doubt that they even existed. I kept quiet about these doubts though. Zara shifted her stance and checked the time as Leo and Bane tinkered with the lock. "Guys, we have 10 minutes to get out of here." She said. "Fuck." Bane said.

There was a clunk from the safe and Leo punched the air. "We're in!" He said as he stepped back from the door. In the safe laid a stack of cash and piles of documents. One pile was labelled ALISHA and had only got two sheets of paper in it. Zara grabbed the documents and whispered, "We have to leave. Now!"

Leo took the stack of cash then turned to follow the rest of us out the back door. Just before we got to the gate we heard the sound of footsteps and "Oi! Stop!" I unlocked the gates and we sprinted to Zara's hover.

As we sped away I said, "That was close. Too close." There was sounds of agreement from both Zara and Bane but Leo was silent. I asked if he ok, then realised he was reading the documents. "What is it Leo?!" My voice became more urgent. "Alisha is in Fuiki. That's a town in the West. One the other side of the continent." There was quiet as we took this in. "Well," said Zara, breaking the silence, "We all have our bags in the boot. Let's set off then."

CHAPTER 9

1 8th of Yaqui 759:

We reached Faytown, a small settlement tucked away in the mountains of Central, 3 days after we left Serilia. Me and Zara jumped off our urka mounts, followed by Bane and Leo. I took the lead as we walked into the centre of the village. There were a few shops with colourful fronts and lots more pop up stalls around the town square. A few people stopped and stared at us and one small girl asked to pet my urka, so we stopped and waited patiently for her to cuddle them.

The was a small bar on the corner of the street that Leo and Bane ducked into, leaving me and Zara with the urka outside. Through the door I could smell the fermented beer and bad incense. There were voices chatting, some breaking into song now and again. I drifted off into a daydream, comforted by the sounds and smells around me.

Too soon, Bane strutted back out, closely followed by Leo. "My contact was there." He smiled. "A stroke of luck." Bane inputted. "He's leaving tomorrow for the capital." "But he says we can stay at his place for a few days." Leo added. "Well that sounds amazing!" I exclaimed, unable to believe our luck. Zara must have been thinking the same as me because she said, "Makes a change from all our bad luck in the past few days."

It was true our luck had been far from good. First we narrowly escaped being robbed by a gang as we entered the rural area outside Serilia, then the hover had been totalled by a joyrider. We all knew how to ride though, with varying degrees of experience. So now we travelled by urka, big beasts with four legs and a tail, covered in scales.

Ours stood around 1.7m high, too small for competition. We wove our way through the market, picking up bits and pieces from some of the stalls. Zoltas money meant we now had £5000 roughly. We had to drag Zara away from a dress store but Leo lingered behind, looking at different rings. I turned to yell to him to hurry up and he finished talking to the owner, hurrying after us.

Leo's friend didn't actually live inside the town borders, as we soon discovered. The house was about 20 minutes out the north side of Faytown, perched on the side of the steep valley. Bane looked bone tired by the time we got inside, bags hanging under his eyes. I didn't think he had been sleeping well since the assassination, but I didn't say any.

I can have that conversation later, I thought. Zara insisted she took the urka round the side to the stables, saying I needed a break from looking after them, so I took the opportunity to explore where we were staying.

Although it didn't look big from the outside the house was actually fairly big. There was the wood and stone front, which is what you saw from the road. It had the dining room, kitchen and a bedroom in it. Behind that was the more cave-like part of the house, hollowed out from the mountain it sat on. All the walls were still the pure rough granite, as was the ceiling on the second floor.

There was a study, bedroom and a library in this part of the house, alongside several rooms that just seemed.... random. I was standing in the doorway of one such room, silently debating whether it was just a room full of odd things or it served some higher purpose when I heard the telltale creak of floorboards.

Two hands looped around me and tugged me into an embrace, whispering, "Guess who?""Leo." Came my reply instantly. That boy was always trying to scare me. "Correct!" He said triumphantly, freeing me from his hug. "Is there a reason you continue to take decades off my life?" I joked."Zara says dinners ready.""Oh good I'm starving.""Same here and I think I smell ambrosia." He said, turning and gesturing for me to follow.

It turned out Leo was right and it was ambrosia Zara was cooking but unfortunately it wasn't for dinner. Instead we had a rabbit stew made with ingredients bought in the market. It was freaking delicious and everyone chatted away merrily in between mouthfuls. Bake told us about a funny mix up at the market earlier, Zara joked we should just stay in this town forever and Leo agreed. Ambrosia was had for dessert, much to Leo's delight.

It was getting late and Bane started yawning. He insisted he wasn't tired, continuing to play poker with us until he actually dozed off. At that point Zara, always the mum, put her foot down, saying we all needed to go to bed. No one argued as it was already 11pm. Me and Leo shuffled off to the second bedroom, wishing Bane and Zara goodnight. This seemed to now be the prearranged sleeping groups and I certainly wasn't complaining.

Practically holding my eyes open I got into my pajamas and brushed my teeth. I was so tired it was untrue. Collapsing into the massive king sized bed I curled into a ball, swiftly drifting off. Just as I was on the edge of sleep Leo sat down on the bed with a thump and curled up behind me, snuggling against me in an attempt to stay warm. It was cold for Yaqui, the summer temperatures not quite here yet. I relaxed into him, dozing off.

CHAPTER 10

1 9th of Yaqui 759:

Feet pounded at the stairs. I awoke with a start, jerking the covers off Leo at the same time. The door flew open. Zara stood, still in her pyjamas, hair sticking up at all conceivable angles. "They're coming." She said, sounding like she was in a state of shock. Still half asleep I replied, "Whose coming?" "A group of the Shadowlords assassins." That woke me up alright. "What!" I nearly screaming, forcing Leo out of his slumber. "Who, what?" He said. "The Shadowlord. Here. Now." I informed him quickly. "Oh shit." "Yep."

I rolled out of bed, feet moving as soon as they hit the floor. "Get dressed, get weapons, then we're getting out." "Yessir!" Zara said, saluting. "Wouldn't it be easier to fortify this place?" Leo questioned as he pulled on a T-shirt. "Nope they probably know where we are. Sooner we bug out, the better."

"Fair point. Let's go." Digging through the suitcase I had been living out of for the past 6 odd days, I recovered a semi-clean white blouse and tight trousers. Throwing those on I pulled a belt tight around my waist, making sure all the attachment points were easily accessible. Hair got swept up into a messy bun, out of the way.

Downstairs toast and mochi lay out, ready to be grabbed and eaten on the go. A pot of coffee sat next to it, alongside some mugs. I poured myself a large cup, aware of Zara's unimpressed look. Bane was standing at the other end of the main dining table, sorting through a pile of equipment. Zara was opposite, first aid kits sprawled out in front of her as she re-organised the contents. "Arya come over here." Called Zara. "You have NPA First Aid right?"

"Yeh I do." I answered, crossing the room to stand by her. Grabbing a handful of mochi and a slice of toast to go with my coffee, I munched as I looked over Zara's shoulder at the kits. Everything seemed well prepared, with just a few key components missing. Those got added quickly, and I clipped one to my belt to check the weight. "That's fine," I said, "Everyone ready to move?" Affirmatives came from the rest of the group.

Me and Bane ran round to the creaking stables, throwing saddles on sleepily urka and loading the huge green beasts up with all our equipment. Being army trained, well sort of, all of us had bug out bags and weapons readily available at all times. Soon we were packed and ready to go. Steadily wondering along the mountainside, I became lulled by the rocking of the urka underneath me. Having had an over privileged upbringing, I had been riding the animals since I could walk, lead and later supervised, by various au pairs. My own mount, Sami, still resided in my parents stables. I might never see her again. I thought, with a twinge of sadness.

"Watch out Arya!" Leo called, concern seeped into his tone. I jerked back to reality and realised my mount was drifting towards the edge of the path. Beneath it lay a 25 meter drop into the river between the mountains. I pulled sharply on the reins, navigating myself back to the wall. "Safe now," I called back. "Thanks!"Leo replied it wasn't a problem and Zara told us to keep a lookout for any signs of an ambush. We all were thinking the same thing. On this path, we're sitting ducks. A sniper could easily take us all out. "30 minutes till we join the main track," Bane called, calming our fears.

Finally, after what seemed like forever, we reached the main track. A 3 car wide path stretched out in front of us, sided by trees. A few birds twittered and flew out as we wondered on, leaving the town and house behind us. I started up a game of I Spy to pass the time, telling the others that the word starts with P. It stared them all in the face, well, if they looked down. "Path?" Bane guessed, after a few non answers. "Nope!" I shouted back cheerfully, pleased to see that I had outwitted them. "It's very obvious," I continued, "We all have one!"

Silence as Zara, Leo and Bane racked their brains for any semblance of an answer. "Just tell us!" Leo called. I headed the group currently, so I swung round in the saddle to answer.

"It was pommel! The front of your saddle!" I said, barely containing my laughter. Leo groaned and smacked his forehead, bemoaning his stupidity. The others laughed like hyenas, cackling. "Well done!" Zara said, "You got us with that!" "My go again?" I asked, jokingly. I knew the answer already. "No way!" Came the collective reply.

Just as Bane opened his mouth to speak, something went screaming over our heads. I whipped round and to my horror, saw 8 black-clad figures moving towards us from the fork in the road, each wearing the Shadowlord's symbol. A 4 pointed black and silver crown. I halted instantly and dismounted. Behind me, I could hear the same actions being undertaken by my friends. I pulled my sword out of its sheath, holding it in the neutral Satara style. Bane stood to my right, Leo and Zara to my left. I gulped. The figures drew their swords and started sprinting towards us.

7v4. The odds were greatly against us. I swung round blocking the first blow. The assassin had a very similar style of fighting to me, but he ignored traditional rules. Swords clashing, we struggled for control until I raised one leg and kicked him back. I followed up with a jab at his ribs but he was out of range. In that second, I knew I was off-balance. He took the advantage, making me jump back as he slashed at my stomach. Around me, I could hear fights going on and swords clashing.

I blocked his blow, twisting underneath his arms. Using him as a support, I jumped raising both my legs and smashing his comrade in the face with the soles of my boots. I landed and swung out of his grasp. We were pressed together. The glint of his eyes showed clearly through the mask. A loud scream sounded behind me....

CHAPTER 11

I whirled round, heart beating its way out of my chest. Leo was still fighting, but Bane stood over a dead assassin, as did Zara. Throwing myself back into the battle with renewed vigour, I swung, blocked and parried with the 2 assassins now trying to kill me. Swinging my sword high, I cut the taller ones throat, fairly severely considering the amount of blood he was losing.

He fell to the ground. This came at a price however. In the second I was distracted, the other assassin took a a lunge at my thigh with a short dagger. Pain shot through my leg as I collapsed to the floor, clutching the wound.

I rolled onto my front, trying to protect my vital organs from the blades. This is it. I thought. I'm going to die. Out the corner of my eye, I could see the sword rising, prepared to cut off my head. There was a muffled groan, then a large thump. A hand rested on my shoulder, gently tugging me. "Arya?" "Yehhh?" I replied, groaning.

Around me, I could hear the sounds of the last few assassins being disposed of."Where are you hit!?" Concern seeped into Zara's tone as she rolled me over."My leg..." I trailed off as she saw the huge gash."Shit, shit, shit, bugger!" A string of profanities left her mouth as Bane appeared in my vision. "Arya, Arya, look at me." He said, putting my head on his knees.

I obeyed, in too much pain to argue. My eyes began to drift shut however, I winced and reopened them when I felt Zara apply a fair amount of pressure to my leg. Leo's voice filtered through. "Hey, hey, I'm here ok? You're going to be ok.""Ok." I replied weakly.

Raising my head off Banes lap, I felt a hand on my back help guide me to a sitting position. Around us the dusty road was stained red and 7 bodies lay crumpled. Zara's hands had worked fast. A rudimentary set of stitches held the cut together. Blood still seeped from it. My vision blurred and I felt dizzy. So tired. I told Bane and Leo this. Both reacted with horror.

"Arya stay with us!" Bane commanded as Leo ran off towards the urka. "I've closed the wound, it's not too deep." Zara's voice rang in my ears."Good." Leo."Here, eat this." Someone held a mochi to my lips. I licked it, then took a bite. Everyone's faces were blurring now. Not good. I swallowed the rest of the mochi, faintly remembering something about how sugar is good for shock. White spots drifted over my vision. Leo sounded increasingly alarmed, but so far away, like I was underwater. I felt water trickle down my front. Everything faded to black...

I could feel myself rocking gently. Something wrapped tight round my waist, digging into the skin above my hips. Voices were muttering all around me but I only caught every other syllable. "Still out...""Blo... loss.""..... rate."

My eyes opened slowly. I saw my urka's head, bobbing slowly as she meandered along. The pain in my thigh came back in a rush. "Fuck." I hissed softly. It felt like someone had taken a hot iron and held it against my leg. "Welcome back." A voice said, sounding relived. Zara."Hi." I replied, my voice stronger than before.I was fully aware now. A rope had been passed round my waist, tying me to Zara, who sat behind me. Leo - leading Zara's urka - rode close by on my left, Bane doing the same on my right.

We kept plodding along as the gang explained what had happened. I had passed out from the blood loss and shock. That much had been obvious. Apparently Zara and Bane struggled to stop the bleeding, resorting to tying a torniquete around my leg and leaving it there for a while. 10 stitches had eventually stopped any blood loss. The only concern now was infection.

I'd obviously been out for quite some time. The battle must've happened around 9am, when the sun had still been relatively low in the sky. Judging by the heat and the position of the sun, I placed it to be around midday. "What are our plans for tonight?" I asked."I'm not sure," Zara replied, "If we don't get to a village by sundown, we're going to have to sleep out."This prospect was dismal.

"Can I see the map?" Leo called. Zara - who had got back on her urka at my insistence that I could ride myself - handed him over the map. Leo dropped his reins to take it and I facepalmed."Leo! Reins!" I called, exasperated. Would he ever learn to ride?! "Sorry!" He smirked, clearly not sorry. I shifted my bad leg slightly to sit more comfortably. In a flash, I doubled over, clutching the wound. Pain stabbed through my leg. Tears sprang to my eyes. "You good?" Bane asked, concerned."Yeh. Give me a second." I hissed between clenched teeth. The pain began to fade and I sat back up.

Leo's face contorted into a frown as the light that filtered through the green leaves danced on his hair. The map was still in his hands and he traced a pattern with his finger. "There's no towns for miles!" He cried. "The nearest is at least 7 hours away!" This was devastating news. We had 5 hours till sundown, max. I took the map back and handed it to Zara. Her jaw clenched tightly shut and she nodded confirmation.

"We're screwed." She announced. "Our food and water supplies won't last us tonight and tomorrow. There's no towns for miles as we're in the middle of the mountain valley and we start climbing again in under an hour. The oxygen at the top of the hill won't be great and we'll suffer from altitude sickness overnight."

"There's definitely no settlements nearby?" Bane asked."No. And I don't want to risk a night on top of a mountain with Arya. She's already hurt and needs a doctor. We should turn back now.""Then we'll get caught!" I protested, pulling my urka over to Zara.

CHAPTER 12

The 19th of Yaqui 759:

I thought Zara might've been right. My eyes were getting heavy and it was becoming harder to see in the twilight. Turning to Bane, the same signs of exhaustion showed on his face. The bags under his eyes were even bigger than before and again I wondered how much sleep he was getting, if any at all.

Before I could ask him, Zara cried out, sounding panicked. "Leo wake up!" The words made me whip round instantly, even though doing this made pain shoot through my leg. Leo sat slumped in the saddle, leaning precariously towards the right. "Leo!" I called. "Leo! Wake up!" This seemed to jolt him awake, eyes squinting at the low sun. "Thanks guys." He replied sleepily.

"Zara I think you were right." I admitted. "We should've turned back.""It's too late now." She replied. "We agreed to keep going, so that's what we have to do.""The lights fading fast." Bane interjected. "Shelter should be our main priority.""I don't see any trees, do you?" I asked, trying to lighten the mood. "No. But that doesn't surprise me, being 2000 metres above sea level." Leo snapped. I went silent for a second. Then said. "Guys we might as well keep going.""Yes." Said Bane. "It's our only choice."

So we kept walking. Every no and then my leg would twinge with pain and we would all have to stop and wait for it to go away. Zara changed the dressing, replacing the blood soaked one with a sterile white bandage. A few of the stitches had ripped and it was bleeding again, but far slower than before. Our progress wasn't quick and tiredness had sunk it claws into everyone. Having got very little sleep last night, only about 5 hours, we were all eager to turn in for the night. But still, no where we could do so. The temperature dropped another 5 degrees and I pulled my coat tighter round me.

Bane had just roused me for a 3rd time when Leo called out. "Lights! Up ahead!""Really?" I replied. "You definitely aren't hallucinating?""No he's not!" Zara cried. "They're right there!"And now I could see them too, clear as day. 4 blocks of yellow light, with others dotted about. "Bane can you check the map?" Flicking on his torch he replied. "There isn't any houses here." "Could it be a trap?" Leo said."Let's find out," I grimaced, pushing my urka forward.

Upon closer inspection the lights did indeed belong to a house. It was very simple. The porch was made out of wood as was the main cabin. Through the windows, we could see two people moving around. Zara jumped off her mount and went to knock on the door. There was a knocker in the shape of a lions head. She hit it a few times, then stepped back. Bane and Leo had got off their mounts as well. The two of them helped down to the ground, making sure my bad leg didn't have too much weight on it. We stood there, cold and hungry waiting for someone to answer the door.

We heard someone moving around inside the house. The door swung inside, revealing a small old woman with curly white hair. "Hello," she said. "what are you young people doing out here at this time of night? Don't you know it's dangerous in the mountains?""Oh, we know." Bane replied. "One of my friends is hurt. Please may we come inside?" He gestured towards me, propped up on Leo. "Of course, dear." She replied. "My name is Ivy. What's yours?""Bane. And this is Leo, Arya and Zara.""Come in, come in." Ivy stepped aside letting us in.

Inside the house is warm, it was such a shock compared to the freezing temperatures we had been subjected to. A fire burned brightly and I could smell something cooking. It was not fancy, the decorations were minimal. But I knew in my heart, we were safe here. Ivy guided us towards several seats, set out in a semi circle around the blazing hearth. While she made sure we were comfortable, a voice called from the next room. "Ivy! Do we have guests?""Yes Denon! 4 young adults, one is hurt." "You're in the living room?" "Yes." "I'll bring some portions of dinner through. It's Hunters Loaf!"

My stomach gurgled at the thought of food. We had ran out at lunchtime. The others looked hungry to. A smiling man in an apron came in, carrying 5 steaming plates of food. "Thank you." We said. The food was piled high. A heap of bright vegetables sat next to 3 slabs of bread, each stuffed with red steak. "Wow!" I exclaimed between mouthfuls. "Where did you get this meat?" "We farm our own animals. Everything on those plates is homegrown." Denon replied, hugging Ivy.

Sitting in the living room with Ivy and Denon, I felt relaxed for the first time in ages. Leo had one arm protectively around my shoulders and Zara rested her head on Bane's. "So, how come you were travelling along this road so late?" Ivy asked. "We're on a mission." I replied, scared to give away too much. "To do what? You all look like you've been in a fight." "We .... Had a run in with some of the Shadowlord's assassins." Bane confided. "You're Resistance?" "We're what?" "Resistance. Against the Shadowlord. That's why me and Denon aren't on the map. We're Resistance so we live off grid."

"We're going to try and take him down." Zara smiled. "Really!?" Ivy exclaimed, shock written all over her kind face. Her blue eyes twinkled with hope. "Yes. We have a contact in Ferrick. Name of Alisha?" I said. "Sorry hun, I've never heard of her." "Oh." Came our collective response. "Here's some contacts we do have in Ferrick." Denon handed us a piece of paper with names and addresses on. "Do any of you remember before the Shadowlord's regime?" Ivy asked, curious."No, the oldest of us is Zara, she's 18.""Let me tell you about when magic was free...."

Ivy took a breath, then continued. "Noxus used to be a place of magic and Fae. That's where your heritage comes from. Those with Fae or Elf blood could harness an energy that flows through the world and use it to do miracles. People would come from far and wide to visit us and experience our culture. Magic was tightly woven into society, but never stopped technology advancing. Diversity flowed and we danced at the equinoxes and solstices for our ancestors and for growth. It was a beautiful time.""Did all with Fae and Elf blood have magic?" Bane asked.

"No, only a select few. Maybe 5% of those populations." Ivy replied before continuing. "I could have only been 20 something when it started to fade, a good 50 years ago. New government policies around magic meant it was restricted. Necromancy could no longer be practiced, even to help find criminals. It wasn't noticeable at first, these restrictions. But slowly, over the years they built up. I lost my magic. Years ago I could grow flowers from a single touch, make the fruit ripen. But this too was outlawed. Then the Shadowlord came to power 15 years ago and cut us off from the outside world. That was when we moved here."

"Wow." I said, amazed. "We never got taught any of that."
"It's a shame. If your generation doesn't learn our history, I
fear it will be lost forever." Denon replied. Noticing that Bane
had begun to drift off, Ivy suggested. "It's getting late. You can
take the two spare bedrooms if you want?""Please." Replied
Zara. "That would be lovely."We went upstairs, following Ivy.
"Goodnight," she said. "I hope you can find Alisha.""We will." I
promised, "We will free magic again."

CHAPTER 13

The 25th of Yaqui 759:

We had been in Ferrick for 3 days now. A member of the underground Resistance, Brogan and his wife Feli, had taken us in to their home. Now in contact with many other members, our main priority is to find Alisha. No one here had ever heard of her but everyone was now engaged in a citywide search. The Shadowlord's presence was minimal to none here and Felicia said that the vast majority of people would fight against him.

Currently I sat in the dining room with Feli, planning next steps. Everyone else had gone out to look for Alisha and I itched to join them, but the wound in my leg made that impossible. So I sat writing a long list of places that Alisha could possibly be living. I put my pen down and sighed. "What's wrong?" Feli asked. "It's not fair! I want to be out doing something! Not stuck here... Writing out addresses!"

"I understand. You're just like Brogan, always wanting to be in the thick of it." She shook her head slightly. "You have to understand Arya. This is important too. If we didn't compile these addresses, our friends wouldn't be able to try find your Alisha.""I guess....." "Your leg needs time to heal. Give it that time and you'll be back in the field in no time."

Finally I finished writing Leo and Banes list. "Done!" I called cheerfully, handing the sheets of paper to Feli. She studied it then laid it down on the pile, smiling slightly. "The others will be home soon. Do you want to do anything?""Will I go round to Sami's and tell them that the meeting will be soon?""Sure darling, remember the safe word is Blue.""You're letting me go for a walk?!" "It's only down the street and back, don't get to excited." Feli laughed.

I pulled on my boots and set off. We were fairly central, in one of the high paying residential areas. All the houses had massive front and back gardens and at least 3 stories. It was a very similar area to were I had grown up in Brogar. The only difference was in this neighbourhood, parents actually seemed to be around. When I was a kid, all my friends had permanent au pairs as their parents travelled for business.

Reaching Sami's house I knocked on the door. A small keypad appeared and I typed in 2583. On this keypad that translated to 'Blue.' Sami opened the door, her black eyes lighting up when she saw me. Sami was part Siren and I still couldn't get over her looks. Her hair shimmered in the light as she stepped outside, followed by Thyr. "How's your leg now?" Sami asked, a brief glint of fangs showing. "Getting better. It doesn't seem to be too badly infected. Feli said it should heal on its own.""That's good. Ready for the dinner party?" "Yep!" I replied brightly. Dinner party was code for Resistance meeting.

It was half an hour into the meeting. As the discussions became less interesting and the topic of conversation wondered straight off into the sunset I sighed. My leg had cramped up again and this meeting was showing no sign of being over soon. I stretched my hand down to massage my muscles, sighing softly as they loosened up.

Thyr and Bane headed up the debate. How fast could we find Alisha? To our dismay the Shadowlord had just passed a decree allowing Resistance movements to be rounded up and executed. Trying to convince us to rein back our search for Alisha was Thyr, while Bane was willing to die in order to find her and take down the Shadowlord.

"It's too risky!" Thyr threw his hands up as he got to his feet."We're so close though!" Bane retaliated. "I can feel it!""Is it worth risking our lives for thought?!""Yes!" Bane screamed this last word, standing up suddenly.

His chair fell over with a clatter. Everyone was silent."Woah guys, I can practically smell the testosterone." Zara said dryly. "I agree," Feli replied. "You two need to stop fighting. We will continue the search for Alisha as Ferrick is considered pretty safe on the whole. That ok?"Both of the guys muttered yes under their breath and sat back down, visibly annoyed at being told off.

A few hours later and Thyr and Sami had left to go home. I sat in the drawing room with Zara, chatting about our days. She had been out on the East side of town with Leo, going round the houses that Alisha might be in. Leo had flopped out over the sofa, long legs swung over one arm with his head resting on the other. I perched next to his head, massaging Leo's scalp while Zara sat on the back of the seat. As I tousled his dark hair, I asked, "Can I come with you guys tomorrow?"

"Oh no." Zara replied. "Not happening darling.""What!? It's the beginning of Litha, please."She sighed and fixed her deep brown eyes on me. Afro bouncing she nodded slowly. "Ok. But only for tomorrow.""Thank you! Thank you!" I screamed jumping up and hugging her tight. "Welcome." She said, wrapping her arms round me. I had been balancing on tiptoe, so when Zara shifted how she was sitting, I overbalanced. Falling into her, she cried out as we toppled over the back of the sofa, landing with a thud on Leo's stomach.

"Ouch." He groaned. "I'm not a landing pad guys." I giggled at this statement. We would have looked a right sight then, limbs tangled. It didn't occur to me that me and Zara, while both fairly petite, might be a bit heavy until he said. "You do realise you two are crushing me?""No, no idea." Zara replied, laughing. The laughter passed onto me and soon both me and Zara were in fits. We stopped when we heard the door open.

"What on Noxus!?" Exclaimed Bane. "We umm, err.... fell over." I stuttered, getting to my feet. He looked at me like I was crazy. "How. Just how." "She hugged me and we overbalanced, landing on Leo." Zara added, brushing herself off. "Hmmm, sure." "It's true!" Leo said. "Fine, fine I believe you. It's time for bed by the way."

CHAPTER 14

2 6th of Yaqui 759:

The door glared at me, practically blinding me with its garish yellow. Shifting my weight, I told Zara, "Would magic users really live here?""How should I know!?""Quiet I think someone is coming to the door." Leo butted in. I stepped off the top step, an old habit that dies hard. After all it is polite to give people some space.

The noise of a chain being released sounded, before the door swung open slightly. "Hello?" A female voice rang out, with a hint of caution."Hello. I'm Arya, this is Zara and Leo. We were wondering if you have someone called Alisha living here?""Well..... Are you Resistance?""Yes." A brash decision to reveal this, but it felt right. The first person to ask after all."Come in." She said.

Pictures hung on the plain blue walls as we were shepherded through into a large dining room. There sat another girl, a pretty one with long white hair and a Southern tan. Sat doing a Cryptex, she looked up, scarlet eyes flashing when she saw me. "Who's this?" She asked, sounding wary of us. "Calm down Lilith, it's Resistance." The first girl soothed. "Wait, really! Are you having a bloody laugh Arden?" "Nope." Arden said. "Sit down you three, I think you've found what you were looking for."

"What." The word fell out of Zara's mouth. "It's a long story, but we are Alisha." Lilith reveals. "But.... Isn't Alisha one person?" Stutters Leo, a look of relief and confusion crossing his face. He was so cute like that. Butterflies did swan dives in my stomach at the sight. "No Alisha is 6 girls. Ali, Lilith, Iris, Stable, Heiki and me, Arden. The first letter of our names spell ALISHA." "Of course! When we got told the name I didn't ever consider it being an acronym!" I groaned at my own stupidity.

The story soon became clear. One by one, the girls joined us round the oak table, sharing information. Each had a very distinct personality, which reflected on their magic, as I got told. Ali bounced about, waving her hands and jumping at every little bit of good news.

She seemed to be the leader and did most of the explaining. A.L.I.S.H.A officially formed back when the Shadowlord had just come to power, but the five wielders had known each other since a very young age. None of the seemed over 25, Heiki barely looked older than me. At one point, Leo's hand snaked into mine and squeezed it tight. Not our secret message or anything, just our fingers laced together.

Each of the girls had their own special magical strength. Magic had been taught briefly at Kocsvo, but in nowhere near enough detail for the three of us to understand everything Sable sung in her pretty East accent. From what I already knew, and what the girls kindly explained for me, Zara and Leo, it went something like this. Each of the girls was in one of the 6 Schools of Magic - Arcane (manipulating energy), Necromancy (communicating and reviving the dead), Nature (harnessing the power of nature) Divination (foretelling the future), Transmutation (changing matter) and Illusion (changing appearance).

As quite possibly the biggest group of wielders anywhere in Noxus, A.L.I.S.H.A is incredibly powerful. Iris told us, twiddling white hair round her finger, "We've never got in contact with the Resistance before. There was a scandal within the magic community, well what's left of it. Some of us got in contact with an underground cell and they got turned in to the Shadowlord by the cell." "What!" Zara sounded completely shocked. "We would never do that!""Agreed." I tried to comfort Iris.

The conversation continued for many more hours. The group had a tower a few hours outside of Serilia, inside a ruined castle. From there they could do most forms of magic that required rituals. Arden and Ali, the two most powerful and therefore those in charge, couldn't be persuaded to meet Feli and the others. "But between the Resistance and A.L.I.

S.H.A we might actually take down the Shadowlord. Please. We'd all be free again." Leo tried to convince Ali. He took her hand in both of his and turned on the charm. It melted me, although I knew it could never be aimed anywhere near me. "Ok. We will meet your cell tomorrow. The park. 10am sharp. I trust you guys." Ali smiled. Jeez. Leo had done well. We left, waving Heiki goodbye.

"Wow." Leo breathed. "That's A.L.I.S.H.A." "Yeh." I replied, massaging my leg as we walked.Zara ran a hand through her hair, sighing. "I just hope they decide to turn up.""Me too. I mean, Leo put on a very convincing act." I punched his arm, laughing."Oh, c'mon, I didn't do anything." He brushed me off, shaking his head."What? Apart from practically ask Ali on a date!?"Zara cackled. We turned onto the Main Street and were instantly swarmed with shoppers and school kids running amok, relishing their freedom. Some not much younger than us.

"I didn't ask her out. I flirted. There's a difference. Besides, I like someone else." "What!!" Me and Zara's jaws dropped. For once, I was at a loss for words. We must've looked completely out of it because he said. "Oh come on, I'm half Elf half Fae! It's not unheard of us to have feelings too!" Leo protested loudly."Who?!" I managed to speak again."Someone I was close to. Very close to.""Was? What do you mean 'was'? Are you not close anymore?" Zara bombarded the poor guy with questions.

"We're still close. But... this, uh, whatever this is.. I think it's changed our relationship." "Ok.... Who?" I asked again as we arrived at Feli's. Zara unlocked the door with a flourish and went in, ignoring us. "I'll tell you later." Leo whispered in my ear, his fingers running along my jaw. The motion set shivers running down my spine. For crying out loud, when did he start to spark this sort of reaction in me! I had been with people before, but never feeling like this.

"Coming inside yet?" Leo and Zara's combined voices jolted me back to reality. "Yeh, just complementing the mysteries of life." I said sarcastically. Closing the door behind me, I heard Feli's voice, "And what time do you think this is!?" Looking at Leo and Zara, I gulped. "Uh oh..." I whispered. "What time is it???" "Ummmmm." Leo looked at his watch. "6...." Feli appeared in the doorway. Her face painted a picture of fury and concern.

"I'm not mad, just disappointed. I hope you have a very good explanation for why you are..." She paused to check the time. "3 hours late back from your shift." "Well... I think everyone should hear this." Zara replied. "It could just turn the tide." "Oh-Kay." Feli looked unsure. "How big is this?" "We could win, big." I blurted out. "We found A.L.I.S.H.A." Feli's mouth dropped. Eyes wide, she smiled. "They're on their way."

CHAPTER 15

2 7th of Yaqui 759:

We sat, or, in Banes case, paced. Zara snapped her fingers and I squeezed Leo's hand tight. Feli ran her hands through her tightly curled locks, shaking them out. We were all waiting for A.L.I.S.H.A to arrive. Thyr cursed as he bit his lip to hard, drawing blood. Even Sami was looking stressed. No one spoke. Everything was riding on today going well. I plaited and un-plaited my bangs with my spare hand. You could practically feel the tension running through the air.

The door bell went. I jumped for the sudden loud noise, and Feli rushed to the door, accompanied by Zara. Leo gently squeezed my hand, once, twice. I turned to look him in the eyes, nearly drowning in their depths. He smiled slightly and turned my head with his other hand so I was once again looking towards the door. I gasped. Standing underneath the wooden frame was Ali, one leg stuck out slightly, emphasising her sky blue skirt.

"Hi.""Hello, Ali, isn't it?" Sami asked, getting out her seat and swanning across the room to shake Ali's hand. Ali smiled graciously, clearly enchanted by the Sirens charm and said, "Yes, and you are?""Sami. Please sit down." The girls sat down around the table. "Hi, Arya!" Ali smiled. "Nice to see you and your boyfriend again."It was then I realised that me and Leo were still holding hands. "Oh she's..." Leo started."We're not together." I said. "Just friends."

Ali gave us a knowing smile and quickly moved on. "Ok, so I'm guessing Zara and the lovebirds filled you guys in on who I am?"I sighed, seeing she was convinced and there was no point arguing. "Yes, they all have a basic understanding." I told Ali."Good, so to go into slightly more detail, I'm Ali, I'm the head of A.L.I.S.H.A and my class is Arcane.""Class?" Thyr asked."Magic class. My proficiency is Arcane magic, so manipulating the elements." Ali explained.

Soon we got down to business. A.L.I.S.H.A could help us, but only from their tower. Maps were dusted off and drawn on, my hands aching from scribbling down notes and directions. Leo dropped an arm round my shoulders, pointing to the map. The journey looked simple, but in reality meant we had to take a treacherous path. The tower itself should be simple once we got there. I would escort A.L.IS.H.A to where they needed to go, thanks to my leg still not being good enough to potentially fight.

Sometime later Bane stood up and said, "I'm hungry, does anyone want lunch?""Yes!" Chorused everyone from round the table."Leo, Arya, run down to the shops with Bane, go get something for lunch.""Is sushi ok with everyone?" Leo asked, "No allergies?" This was directed to Ali."Yeh, sushi's good." Ali said."Cool. Bane do u want to get stuff ready here, me and Arya can hand,e the shopping?""Sure. If you two need some alone time.""No... we're... we're not a... a couple." I sighed. Leo said nothing, however. Interesting.

Grabbing a handful of cash out the change jar, I shouted through, "We'll be back in 10!""Cool!" Feli shouted back.Leo produced a key from his pocket, locking the door behind us as we stepped outside into the blinding sun. I shoved a pair of sunglasses on my face, blinking in relief. It must've been at least 30C out here. "C'mon, let's get going before we cook.""Don't exaggerate Arya." Leo rolled his eyes, but pulled off his hoodie.

Conversation tailed off until Leo said."So you know that girl I liked?""Yesss...." Butterflies did flips in my stomach."I don't know how you're going to react to this but it's..""Yes?""You." "What! I'm.. you... you like.... Me!" I was in shock. Surely this was some sick joke."Yeh. Do you like me?""Yes."

My jaw dropped. For so long I had secretly liked him, keeping my feelings tucked away so we could remain friends. And now he liked me back! It was a miracle. Before I could say anything else, he pushed open the glass door to the shop and said, "After you?" We entered and quickly rounded up the groceries we needed. Small talk was made, but I felt uncomfortable broaching the subject of girl/boyfriends. Just cause we liked each other didn't mean we were together. And with everything happening around us, I felt like a relationship could be an inconvenience.

Opening the door, I shouted, "We're home! And have sushi!" "Yesss!" Feli squealed, her childish side showing through. Graciously I handed her a packet, setting the others down on the table. I grabbed a packet for me before they all disappeared, and, on an afterthought, grabbed one for Leo too. He smiled slightly as I handed it to him, but his green eyes twinkled. That was rare.

You could barely see the table anymore. Swamped by maps, notebooks and takeout cartons, we would need to tidy up before anything got done. Thyr licked sauce off his fingers, eyes closed. Sami's perfect fangs showed under the curl of her lips. Zara jokingly pushed vegetables into Banes face, laughing as the taller Southerner squirmed away. For a moment, I could fool myself. We were back at Kocsvo, pissing around on the sports field during our afternoon free, enjoying the sun.

Reality sunk in as we finished lunch, papers got cleared into the kitchen bin, and we got back to work. Finally, the final version was ironed out. At 0900 hours we would meet at A.L.I.S.H.A's house. By 1130 hours our groups should be at the tower. At 1300 hours, we should be on our way home. It seemed simple enough, but I had a horrible feeling some-thing was going to go badly wrong. As we let Ali out, thanking her for coming, a single crow cawed in the tree.

CHAPTER 16

3 2nd of Yaqui 759:

Crouched by the tree, I saw Bane signalling over to me. Come here. Rolling my eyes, I checked that no one was watching as I dashed over, grass rippling against my calves. I huffed. "What is it!?""Look. Over there." Bane pointed into the far distance. I squinted, but couldn't make anything out. "There's nothing there." I said, my voice a low whisper as I tucked a loose strand of hair behind my ear. The only things I could see were the rippling grass plains and animals grazing on the gentle slope of the other hill.

"There's nothing there Bane." I sighed. "You're paranoid, that's all.""No, there definitely is!" His voice raised slightly and I shushed him. "Dear, I can't see anything. Nothings there.""D on't patronise me, I'm older than you." "Fine. Wait I think I've seen it." I had to admit, now I could see something moving.

Bane signalled to everyone, making them run to the wire fence we were at. "Look guys, over there." "Oh-Kay..." Zara whispered. "Who is that?" "We're not sure." I said. "I have a bad feeling though." "Let's continue. Very slowly." Arden advised. We agreed and got up, setting off again.

I took in the scenery. Clear blue skies and a light breeze, the sun shining down. We had rejoined a cobbled road, the dusty rocks a contrast to the bright green and yellow fields. A plentiful harvest, or so it seemed. I knew that many people would never see their share. The rich and the powerful would get plenty, while the commoners starve. In the distance, I saw the ruined tower rise up from the top of a gently rolling hill. Only an hour and a bit left.

"Beautiful, isn't it?" Iris fell into pace beside me. The petite girl had long black hair, currently swept back in a thick plait. Her chocolatey eyes ran over me, waiting for a response. "Yes. It really is." I replied. "I remember when the fields here still held forests. A long time ago, now." "Yeh..." I had almost forgotten that these girls were actually in their late 60s, even though they barely looked 20. It was how wielders aged apparently. 60 to us was around 25 to them.

"Guys? You know how we saw those people earlier...." Zara's voice trailed off. "Yes?" My stomach knotted with anxiety. Feeling nauseous, I continued. "Is there a problem?" "Well.... You could say that." Leo butted in. "Spit it out." I sighed. "I think we're being followed. By the Shadowlord." "What!!" A collective scream of horror rose, before being quickly shushed by Feli.

"Give me the binoculars." I said, panicked. This couldn't be happening. Not now. We had come so far. My fingers struggled to grip the focusing the knob, shaking and slipping. Finally, everything went from blurry to crystal clear. And yes, Leo and Zara were spot on. What looked like a battalion marched steadily over the plain towards the castle. "No." I whispered, passing the binoculars back. "We can't let this stop us. We're so close."

"It's too risky." Feli argued. "We can't risk a massacre." "It's not a huge amount, we'll be able to take them!" Leo piped up."We contacted other rebels, didn't we? Surely some will have turned up?" Bane asked."Maybe, it's a big ask." Thyr said. "As long as the basic plan remains the same, we'll be fine." Heiki replied, running a hand through her red hair and tying it up.

It was agreed then. On we went, stopping to take a break only when my leg started to ache. I rested under the shade of a large tree, leg stretched out. Bane sat beside me, munching on a sandwich. "So... how's you and Leo?" He asked, smirking.I spluttered. "What!?" "Oh, c'mon it's obvious to anyone with two working eyes and a brain.""Well... um... it's... we got to the part we tell each other we like each other and... not much further." I confided, massaging my leg with my hands.

"So, you're together?" Bane prodded."I'm not sure." He sighed. I felt the urge to question him about why he had never had a girlfriend before. Why he'd never shown any interest at all. I turned to look at him. Bane's eyes still had dark bags under them, but they had a shine to them that they hadn't since the assassination. I was glad to see this. Before I could open my mouth and speak, he smirked and called out, "Hey! Leo!"

"What are you doing?!" I hissed. My cheeks flushed bright red. Leo sauntered over, one hand resting casually on his gun. "Hey." He replied. "What do you need me for?""Arya has something to say to you." Bane said in a rush. "Oh-Kay." Leo drawled. "Um, I, I think, uh.... Well we talked about,uh, liking each other so maybe we could, you know, go on a date sometime?" I stammered, tripping over my words as I twirled my bangs round and round.

"Yeh. Sure I would really like that." Leo smiled at me. I opened my mouth to speak, but Sami's voice cut across the air. "C'mon guys, let's get moving!" We jumped up, Leo offering his hand to help pull me to my feet. I took it, still annoyed my leg wasn't fully healed yet.

CHAPTER 17

3 2nd of Yaqui:

We were here. The tower loomed above me, crumbling and ruined. From the other side of the field, the Shadowlord's army came running towards us. A stringy group at best. At least a 100 fighters from different parts of Noxus had gathered, here after they heard about A.L.I.S.H.A. All seemed fully confident with their weapons, but some were massively underweight and I privately held some doubts about their ability to fight a fully trained an staffed army.

"Arya, you, Sami and Valeria are going with A.L.I.S.H.A to the tower. The rest of us will stay and fight off the N.A, try buy you some time." Feli said quickly, stealing glances at the approaching soldiers. I opened my mouth to argue that Leo wasn't with me. Suddenly he was by my side, arm round me. "Hey, it'll be ok, I'll be right here to catch you after we beat these fools." His hot breath tickled my ear. "You sure?""Yes. Remember, I'll always wake up." He planted a soft kiss on my cheek before turning away and joining the main group, seamlessly slipping in.

Feli and all looked at me in shock, but before any of them could open their mouths, a cry went up. "Move out! Move out!" "Go." Feli shouted, turning round. The 9 of us sprinted in the open door, feet echoing up the stairwell as we pounded through the foyer and up the main stairs. It was surprisingly roomy inside, but as we ascended, it got narrower and more ruined.

The first sounds of battle could be heard from outside. Screams of pain and triumph. I tried to concentrate. All the girls were busy prepping while us soldiers stood guarding the door. I took in the room. Massive symbols were painted onto the walls. Dust sheets covered pieces of obscure furniture. Iris pressed down on a trapdoor, revealing massive jars of salt and crystals. Long scrolls of paper were next. A perfect white and black quill with a pot of ink.

Everyone seemed to have a job to do. Ali sprinkled salt in a large circle. Iris wrote in illegible handwriting, a language I had never seen before. Arranging crystals was Sable. A crash sounded from downstairs. Shit. Had someone broken the door down? I ran to the window and peered out through the thick layers of grime. There was a seething mass of people, but I couldn't make out who was on whose side.

"Arya? I think we might have a break-in issue." Valeria's thick accent causing her to pronounce my name as A-ray-a instead of A-ree-a. I turned to reply. "What do ya mean?""There's people downstairs.""Fuck buggery. Valeria, stay here, make sure these six get to complete their tasks. Sami, with me."

After a few seconds of odd looks, I clapped my hands. "C'mon, get moving people!"Sami jumped and pulled the door open. I followed her out the room, telling the others good luck as I shut the door behind me. We crept down the stairs. I held my breath, scared to make any noise that could alert the intruders of our presence. Sami produced a periscope from her leather bag and checked round the corner at the bottom of the second flight of stairs.

"It's them." She signed. I nodded grimly, hands flying as I signed back, "You take the left, I'll take the right."Her thumb and forefinger made a circle as she replied, "Ok." She ran to the other side of the corridor. I poked my head round the corner and watched the 4 N.A soldiers. Each was fully armed and carrying either a gun or a sword visibly. I gulped, knowing full well that a variety of hidden weapons would also be on their person.

3, 2, 1. Sami counted down, drawing her small pistol that was similar in size and shape to the ones that we trained with. I pulled out my long sword. It hissed as I slipped it out the sheath. Studying the soldiers weak points, I noticed that their necks and hip area were exposed due to joints in the armour. Communicating this, I took a tentative step forward.

All the soldiers looked as though they were studying a map, or book of some sort, standing in a tight circle looking down.

Weird. But it gave me and Sami a huge advantage. In sync with each other, we snuck up behind the closest two, weapons drawn. I raised my sword. And swung. Blood sprayed out as the neck got cut in two, revealing the glistening tendons and bones. I was instantly covered in red, as was Sami, her pale skin speckled with crimson blood.

The other two had noticed. They drew their weapons, swords, and swung at me and Sami. I blocked, sidestepped, and swung low. He jumped back, making me off balance. Seizing the opportunity, he hit the side of my injured leg with the flat of his sword, knocking me to the floor. Using the momentum, I rolled over backwards and jumped back to my feet, ignoring the warm wetness spreading from my leg. I jumped, using a roundhouse style kick to disarm him.

I thought he was unarmed now, only to find him pulling a short dagger from his boot. I hit his chest, winding him. As he staggered back, Sami shot at the second enemy, killing him. Just one to go now. He ducked as I aimed for his head, only to find my good foot kicking him backwards onto the cold hard stone floor. I wobbled slightly, but quickly righted myself and used the tip of my sword to keep him still while Sami finished him off.

"Let's get back to the others." I whispered. "Yeh. I'll seal the door first." "Ok." I started back up the stairs, wincing when the weight shifted to my bad leg. Blood was seeping from my wound where the stitches had broken. Finally I reached the top room.

It was an... interesting sight. Definitely. Through the little window in the top of the door, I could see Ari and Sable with their arms flung up in the air. A large crystal glowed bright blue. "And you are standing outside because..." I asked Valeria. "Can't have anyone who isn't magical in the room. Could kill us. In theory." She explained. I had my doubts but ok.

Sami pounded up the stairs. "Wha..." She didn't get a chance to finish her sentence. Bright blue light streamed out the room, from the window and the cracks around the doors. I covered my eyes, staggering back into Valeria. A blast had physically pushed me back. A scream rose from outside.

After what seemed like an age the light disappeared and the door swung open. All the girls were collapsed on the rough wooden floor, looking exhausted but happy. "We won." Iris said, smiling softly. My face lit up and I ran over and hugged Iris. Everyone else piled in. Tears of joy ran down my face, and we jumped up and down. It was over. Finally.

I noticed Ali hadn't rejoined the group. "Are you ok?" I asked, detangling myself from the others. "I'm so sorry Arya." Ali's face turned serious as she turned towards the group. "Leo's gone."

Epilogue

The 32nd of Yaqui:

Screaming and sobbing, I ran from the tower onto the battlefield. The information Ali got was false. It had to be. Dodging the remains of the defeated Shadowlords army I ran to where Zara was kneeling on the ground, bending over someone. I looked around, desperate to see Leo standing near her. He wasn't there. It was Bane that crouched a few metres away, dealing with an injured Resistance fighter.

NO! I thought as I approached Zara and saw who she was treating. Leo, my Leo, was lying on his back, a bloom of blood across his chest. I sprinted the last couple of metres, ignoring the stabbing pains in my leg and knelt next to Zara. "Is he going to be okay?!" I fretted. There was a pause. I knew instantly the answer. A fresh wave of tears started streaming down my face, making clean streaks run through the grime and blood.

"Hey..." murmured Leo as he woke up. "It's ok. I'm here." "Leo," I cried, cradling his body in my arms, "Leo I can't lose you." At this point Zara stood up and backed off, sensing we needed to be alone. "Oh Arya," began Leo, "You are the best thing that's ever almost happened to me." "Then let's make it happen. We can go back to Serilia, have 3 kids and grow old together. You're going to be ok Leo."

He paused then whispered. "We both know that's a lie." "I can't lose you Leo!" "I'm... I'm so sorry Arya" "Leo.... I know it to late to say it but... I love you. I love you more than anything else in this world and I'm only realising it now I'm going to lose you and it's not fucking FAIR!"

"Life isn't fair Arya. Goodbye..." "Leo don't go. I need you. I LOVE YOU!" My voice cracked. "I need to say something. You've always meant the world to me. And it's too late now but Arya Winters... I..."

A single tear trickled out of the corner of his perfect green eyes. I heard him take a deep breath, exhale, a flicker of a smile on his lips and his eyes glazed over. "Leo. No Leo. No it's not fair," I cried. "You promised me you would wake up! Please Leo! One more miracle. You told me you'd wake up. You bastard wake up!" I slapped him. "You selfish bastard WAKE UP!"

I sat there, sobbing and shaking, cradling his head in my lap. I just couldn't believe it. Leo, my Leo, who always survived, even when it was impossible, was gone. Dead.

Zara crouched next to me and put her arm around my shaking shoulders. "Come on. There's nothing you can do for him now. Medical can take him back inside." She hiccuped. I noticed she was crying too, tears flowing freely from her eyes.

"NO!" I screamed, throwing her arm off me, "ITS NOT FAIR!" I ran out of breath by the end and finished in a whisper. My energy left me and I slumped, only supported by Zara. "Hey, Arya, talk to me." She said, voice thick with tears. "Arya, please, say something." There was nothing to be said. I couldn't form words. Just mindlessly sob and howl.

Bane spoke. "Arya? I'm so sorry." The voice barely filtered through the white noise in my head. My voice had completely stopped. It was over. But I had lost Leo. The thought made me howl in pain. This couldn't be happening. People were moving around me, but the pictures didn't register in my head. I had stopped crying too. The only noise I made was the sound of breathing. Like I had been switched off.

Zara laid Leo's head gently on the ground as I curled up in a little ball, snivelling and sobbing, my face a mess of tears, snot, blood and mud. So Zara picked me up like you would a baby and carried me back to ALISHAs tower, Bane following with Leo in his arms. I buried my head in Zara's chest, passing out.

Milton Keynes UK
Ingram Content Group UK Ltd.
UKHW020024271124
451585UK00013B/1447